GHOST
MOUNTAIN

ANNE SCHRAFF

red rhino
b⬤⬤k s®

With more titles on the way ...

SADDLEBACK
EDUCATIONAL PUBLISHING
www.sdlback.com

Copyright ©2015 by Saddleback Educational Publishing
All rights reserved. No part of this book may be reproduced in any form or by any means, electronic or mechanical, including photocopying, recording, scanning, or by any information storage and retrieval system, without the written permission of the publisher. SADDLEBACK EDUCATIONAL PUBLISHING and any associated logos are trademarks and/or registered trademarks of Saddleback Educational Publishing.

ISBN-13: 978-1-62250-897-6
ISBN-10: 1-62250-897-1
eBook: 978-1-63078-029-6

Printed in Guangzhou, China
NOR/0116/CA21600037

20 19 18 17 16   2 3 4 5 6

Winston

Age: 11

Favorite Food: lamb stew

Best Skills: shooting video game aliens and drawing with marker pens

His Dog's Name: Smoky Joe

Best Quality: can admit when he's wrong

CHARACTERS

Age: around 14 (when he died)

Favorite Food: bighorn sheep stew

Best Skills: shooting a bow and arrow and mixing paint colors from berries and leaves

His Horse's Name: Floating Smoke

Best Quality: friendliness

1
MAN UP

"Winston Lawson," Dad yelled in his big voice. "What're you doing, boy? You've been in that room for two hours."

← alien warriors

"I'm playing a cool game, Dad," Winston yelled back. "*Doomscape*. The alien warriors got us cornered. We got these new lasers. My friend from school is playing on his laptop too. But I'm helping our guys more."

Winston was eleven. He was in sixth grade. There was nothing he liked more than playing action games. He played on his laptop and cell phone.

Dad's normal voice

"The sun is shining out there," Dad shouted. Dad never talked in a low voice. He talked loud. He talked very loud when he was angry. Like now. "Sun shining. Birds singing. Folks out on bikes. Jogging. Shooting hoops. Some of them walking their dogs. It's Saturday. No school. What're you doing playing silly games in your room?"

Dad swung open the door to his oldest

son's room. "Hey, Winston, shut that thing off. Get moving!"

"But, Dad," Winston groaned. "We're in the middle of a game. I'm winning. The aliens are on the run."

"Shut that thing off. Get moving, boy. Or you're gonna be on the run from me," Dad shouted again.

Mom came down the hall. "Oh, honey, give Winston a break. He's done all his chores. He's been doing his homework," Mom said. "No harm in him having a little fun." Mom was a lot nicer than Dad. Winston thought so anyway. He wished Dad was more like Mom.

"Bella," Dad said. "The boy likes adventure, right?"

"Yes, he's playing his favorite adventure game," Mom said. "It's called *Doomscape*."

"Yeah," Winston said eagerly. He hoped Mom was winning Dad over. "It's really exciting."

"I like adventure too," Dad said. "Adventure in the real world. Climbing hills. Meeting wildlife. Crawling over rocks. Getting sore and dirty. That's what we're doing today." He pointed at Winston. "You. Me. And your brother, Nelson. I got the truck all packed. Sandwiches, fruit, cold drinks."

"Awww, Dad," Winston groaned.

"Come on, boy. Get your jeans on. Your hiking shoes. I just bought them for you. The great outdoors is calling," Dad said. He walked down the hall to his younger son's room. "Nel! Nelson," he shouted, knocking on the door. "What's up, boy?"

Nelson's door

"I'm sleeping," Nelson said in a groggy voice. "It's Saturday. No school." Nelson was eight years old. He was in third grade.

"Sleeping? At this hour of the morning?" Dad yelled. "Up and at 'em, boy. We got big plans. You. Me. Winston. We're going to have an adventure. Put on your jeans. Your hiking shoes. You boys are going to man up today. And in a big way."

DAD'S PLANS
for Nelson and me ::

1. Have an ADVENTURE!
2. Teach boys to MAN UP
3. Ask who shaved the cat!

It was Nelson ←

2
BUNNY ATTACK

Mom was in the hall behind Dad. "I'm worried. Boys as young as Winston and Nelson hiking in wild places. I mean, it can be dangerous in the hills. What with snakes and wild things. One little slip? You can be badly hurt. They're just little boys," she said.

Mom's worst nightmare

"Bella, I went hiking with my dad. And my brothers. *And* my sisters in Arkansas when I was four years old! Four freakin' years old. We're raising wimpy couch potatoes. I won't stand for that. I want strong boys. Outdoor boys. With a feel for nature. I don't want them playing video games twenty-four seven. Hiding in their rooms. Sleeping away the day."

"Where are you taking them hiking?" Mom asked. She still looked worried. She grew up in the city. Mom's idea of wildlife was a chipmunk in the front yard. "I don't want the boys falling off a cliff. I don't want them attacked by wildlife."

Angry ← chipmunk

"Bella, we're going to the Anza Borrego Desert. Nice easy trail. Maybe a couple bunnies. But I'll protect the boys if they attack. I mean, I know those bunnies got big teeth. But we'll be okay. I never heard of a bunny eating a boy."

"Now you're making fun of me," Mom grumbled.

Luke Lawson was a big, burly man. He looked a bit mean. But his eyes danced when he smiled. He looked jolly. Now, he grinned. And grabbed Mom. He swung her around.

Dad really digs mom

"Girl, I love those boys with all my heart. I'll bring them home safe and sound. Promise," Dad said.

Winston came slowly from his room. "I hate this," he said.

"That's too bad," Dad said. "You know what I hate? I hate a boy of mine wasting his time on stupid video games. You know why I named you Winston?"

Winston rolled his eyes. "Yeah, Dad. You told me a million times. Some fat, old English dude. Winston Churchill. Died a million years ago," Winston said.

"You just got an F in history," Dad said. "Winston Churchill was a great man. He helped save the world from evil. And I named your brother for Nelson Mandela. Because Mandela suffered so much to bring freedom to his people. They were great men. They were active. They didn't waste their time playing stupid games. They were doers. These are your heroes. Not comic book freaks in video games."

POW! ZAP! ← this didn't happen

An hour later, the three of them were in the truck. They were heading east.

"I hate these jeans," Winston said. "They're stiff as boards."

"Yeah, mine too," Nelson said. "And these shoes hurt my feet."

"What's the stupid place we're going to?" Winston asked.

"The Anza Borrego Desert. And it's not stupid," Dad said.

"The desert?" Nelson said. "I bet there's a bunch of rattlesnakes out there. Just waiting for us."

"I hate snakes," Winston said. "They make my skin crawl."

"They hate you too," Dad said. "Snakes are *more* afraid people."

"We'll die out there," Nelson moaned. "I can see the story on TV. Three die in desert from snakebites."

3

COUCH POTATOES

"It's hot in the desert," Winston said. "People die in the heat. I'm sick already just thinking about it."

"It's only March," Dad said. "It's not hot."

"There's nothing to eat out there," Nelson said. "We'll starve."

"There's enough food in the ice chest to feed an army," Dad said. "Man, this hike is overdue. You two are lazy whiners. You're soft, boys. You need to man up so bad."

Want some cheese with your whine?!

"In the mountains, we could find wild berries. Or something," Winston said.

"Oh, we can find wild seeds. We can pound them into flour," Dad said.

The boys looked grossed out. Their eyes were big.

"I don't want to pound seeds into flour," Nelson said.

Dad laughed. "We've got lots of food. We'll only be gone five or six hours. You can stuff yourselves. There are sandwiches and cookies."

"You mean we gotta hike for six hours?

My feet hurt already in these ugly shoes," Winston griped. "Dad! It'll kill us. We'll drop dead."

"We'll be hiking for an hour. Maybe," Dad said. "If you can't make it back, you can piggyback down to the trailhead."

"I hate this so much," Nelson said.

"Know what I hate?" Dad yelled. "Whiny couch potatoes. In an hour from now, we'll be seeing great stuff. The Kumeyaay people used to live out here. They left beautiful art. They harvested berries. Made them into mush."

Berries inside

"What's mush?" Winston asked.

"Like cereal. Like oatmeal. Sort of," Dad said.

"I hate oatmeal. I like pancakes. And syrup. And lots of butter," Nelson said.

"Yeah," Dad said. "That's why you're putting on weight. Getting out of shape. Gotta do something about that. You guys need this hike. Toughen you up. Make you lean. I've been planning this for a long time."

Need to
get in shape

"When will we get there?" Winston asked. "It seems like we've been driving forever.

I'm thirsty too. You got something to drink in that cooler?"

"We've been driving for an hour. And we'll be there in about forty minutes," Dad said. "But I'm a nice guy. I'll pull over. Get you guys some cold orange juice."

"No soda pop?" Nelson asked.

"You guys drink too much of that," Dad growled. He pulled the truck off the highway. "Don't make me mad." Then he got out of the truck. He went to the back. Then started looking in the ice chest.

Winston turned to his brother. "I'm so bored!" he said.

"Me too," Nelson said. "I wish this horrible day was over. I hate this. And we got that hike ahead of us. My feet hurt just thinking about it."

Winston looked out the window. That's

when he saw it. A huge snake. Right where Dad was standing. It was crawling out from behind a rock.

4

SNAKE!

"Dad! Look out!" Winston shouted. "There's a snake by your foot!"

Dad jumped. The boys had never seen him jump so high.

"Whoa," he shouted. "That's a rattlesnake there. Big fella too. Just woke up from a nap, I guess." Dad looked up into the cab of the truck. "Good heads-up, Winston."

"Let's go home," Winston groaned. "I knew there were snakes here."

← Mom buys organic

Dad laughed. He got three icy bottles of orange juice from the chest. "These will make us all feel better," he said. He handed them the juice. Then he downed one himself. "That old snake wasn't rattling. He wasn't looking for trouble. Snakes are shy unless you surprise them."

"I hate snakes. I hate the desert too," Nelson said.

"Put a lid on it," Dad said. "We got some miles to go. There will be a dirt road. That's the start of our trail."

"Dirt road?" Winston said. "What if we get stuck?"

"Driving on a dirt road is gonna be awful," Nelson said. "This is an old truck. We bounce on smooth pavement."

"Come on," Dad said. "This is a pretty cool old truck. Thousands of miles on it. Still going strong."

← Dad's truck

"I could be home now. Playing video games. Chillin'," Winston said. "But I'm stuck here with dangerous snakes. Dad, this is cruelty to kids. I'm only eleven."

"What about me?" Nelson said. "I'm only eight!"

"Snap out of it! This is a little hike. One

mile up. One mile back. Easy trail. Almost no slope. You won't even know you're climbing. Stop complaining. You'd think we were climbing Mount Everest," Dad said.

Mt. Everest is 29,029 feet high!

"Trailhead up there. There's the parking lot. We're here!" Dad sounded excited. "Everyone out."

"Nobody else is here. I don't see any cars," Winston said. "Nobody else is crazy enough to come here."

A sign read Ghost Mountain Trail.

"You know what that means," Winston said. "This place is haunted. Ghosts! Boo!"

Dad laughed. "Ghosts only come out at

night. We'll be gone before it gets dark."

Nelson looked at several rocks. They had strange markings on them. They looked like bird's feet. "What's this stuff?" he asked.

"Kumeyaay art. It's beautiful," Dad said. "It's all over. Just look. Everywhere. You'll see different designs."

The guys moved toward the trailhead. The boys had to admit it looked easy. There was hardly a slope. They started hiking.

"Look at those weird rocks," Nelson said. "They got round holes in them. What's with that?"

Dad pulled out his cell phone. He

started taking pictures. "That's where the Kumeyaay folks pounded seeds into flour. Keep your eyes open, you guys. We're coming up on some really great art."

There were black lines. They looked like stick figures.

"What do the pictures mean?" Nelson asked.

"Nobody knows," Dad said. They passed a hillside. There were green agaves. Dad took more pictures. "The Kumeyaay people used agave for food, medicine, rope."

"Wow. Those pictures would be good for a school report," Winston said. "My teacher would like that."

The boys looked at each other. They frowned. They didn't want their dad to think they liked hiking. No way!

"We're about to turn around. Head back," Dad said.

"That's it?" Winston asked.

"Yeah," Dad said. "Now that wasn't so bad. Was it?"

The boys didn't answer. The walk back seemed to go fast. Easier. They saw the truck.

"Ready. Set. Go," yelled Nelson. He took off. Winston was right behind him. He didn't want his little brother to win. He wanted to get back to the truck first.

Dad walked back to the truck. He was grinning. But he didn't say anything. He got out the ice chest. They all ate sandwiches. Then salad. And fruit. They drank iced tea.

After eating, they climbed into the truck. It was time to go home.

"We should be home before dark," Dad said.

Then it happened. The engine wouldn't start. Dad spent a few minutes looking at it. But he couldn't get it working.

"The truck's dead," Nelson cried. "We're sunk!"

"Oh man," Winston groaned. "Ghost Mountain. It's cursed. We should have known better. I knew it! I knew something bad would happen. We aren't going home."

5

ENJOY IT

"Hold on," Dad said. "Don't freak out, guys. This is just a little bump in the road."

He called Mom on his cell phone. "Bella, we're having a little engine trouble. Nothing to worry about—"

"The truck's dead. We're stuck! We're in the middle of nowhere," Nelson shouted.

"Don't pay any attention to him. It's all good, Bella. We had a great hike. The lunch was tasty. But I gotta call a tow truck," Dad said calmly. He gave Nelson a dirty look. Put his finger to his lips.

"Where are you?" Mom cried.

"We're at the Ghost Mountain Trail. But don't worry. We'll be fine. We have plenty of food and water. A tow shouldn't take too long," Dad said. "They can figure out what's wrong. Then we'll get on the road."

need to
← call this
guy

"Is the forest ranger there?" Mom asked.

"No, this is just a little place," Dad said. "Too small for a ranger."

"Just snakes," Nelson hissed. He didn't

want Mom to hear. Dad's phone picked up everything.

"It'll be dark in a few hours." Mom was worried.

"Don't worry. Even if we have to stay the night. We came prepared. We got sleeping bags. We'll just sleep in the truck. Wait it out. It'll be an adventure. The sky is crazy clear. We'll stargaze. See the Milky Way. It'll be amazing."

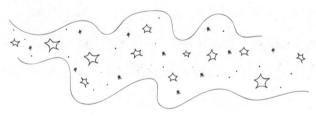

Winston knew his dad. Dad loved this stuff. Loved being outside. Loved camping. Maybe Dad did something to the truck. He rolled his eyes. Groaned. He would have to suck it up.

Dad said good-bye to Mom. He was all smiles. Then he called for a tow truck. The guy said they were swamped. They would get there after dawn.

"You guys," he said. "This is gonna be great. Something you'll remember."

"I don't want to be here in the dark," Nelson cried.

"Yeah," Winston said. "What if some wild animals come?"

"Or snakes," Nelson said. "They'll bite us in our sleep. We'll die!"

"Snakes don't crawl inside trucks," Dad said. "They slither on the ground."

"I saw this movie. It was about a monster.

It lived in the Anza Borrego Desert. Right around here. It was called the Sandman," Nelson said. "It was huge. Its claw tracks were seven feet apart. It tore things to shreds."

"Movies aren't real. You're too old to believe that, Nelson. Mostly bighorn sheep around here. They don't bother anybody."

"I bet there are wolves. And wildcats," Winston said.

"Just calm down. Enjoy our adventure," Dad said. "The sunset will be amazing. We can take pictures."

"Why do they call it Ghost Mountain?" Nelson asked.

" 'Cause there are ghosts out here, Nel." Winston grinned.

"Knock it off," Dad said.

"I wish we were home," Nelson said. "Mom was going to make pasta tonight. With meatballs. My favorite."

I like extra sauce

"What about the big game? It's on tonight," Winston said.

"Come on," Dad said. "Let's explore."

6
CAMP OUT

Later, it was time to unroll the sleeping bags.

Nelson climbed into the truck. He touched the first bag. "There's a snake! Right here in my sleeping bag. It's waiting for me to crawl inside."

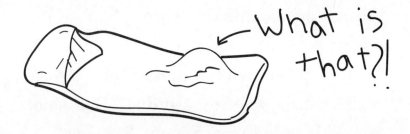

What is that?!

"Bet it's one of those rattlers," Winston said.

Dad jumped into the bed of the truck. He shoved Nelson away. Dad shook the bag. A large lizard appeared. It leaped off the truck. Then raced across the sand and disappeared.

"Just a poor little lizard." Dad laughed. "Shame on you. Making such a fuss over a lizard."

"Well, it looked like a snake," Nelson said.

"This trip was *way* overdue," Dad said. "You kids need to toughen up. Big-time."

The sun went down. The sky was red. Purple. Pink. The hills turned gold. Then the stars came out. More stars than the brothers had ever seen.

Nelson ruined the moment. "I can just taste Mom's dinner," he whined.

"I can smell her homemade apple pie," Winston said.

Extra apples

Dad's phone rang. He picked up. The boys could tell who it was. Mom again. They could hear her voice loud and clear.

"You guys okay?" she asked.

"We're fine. We're eating those extra sandwiches you made. And we're having peanut butter cookies for dessert."

"Let me talk to the boys," Mom said. Winston was first. "How are you doing, honey? I miss you so much."

"Oh, Mom. I wish we were home. It's awful here. Snakes and—"

Dad grabbed the phone. "No snakes, Bella. There was a lizard. These kids … I'm telling you. Our boys need this. Their brains are mush."

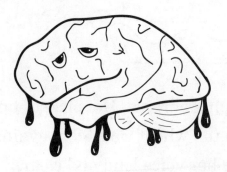

The guys got into their sleeping bags. The truck bed was crowded. Dad was sound asleep first.

Winston tapped Nelson. "You sleeping?"

"No," Nelson said. "I miss my bed."

There was a humming sound. "What's that?" Winston asked.

"A bug," Nelson said. "Everything's bad out here. Probably got killer bugs too."

Winston sat up. Looked around. Then he saw a shape. It was near some rocks. He grabbed Nelson. "There's something out there! It's moving. By those rocks. I think it's coming this way."

Both boys shoved their father hard.

"Dad! Wake up!" Winston shouted. "I see something. Over there. And it's coming this way."

Dad sat up. He grabbed a flashlight. Looked around the trailhead. "I don't see anything."

"Somebody is standing over there. Look by the rocks," Winston cried.

Nelson chimed in, "What if it's the Sandman?"

"I don't see anything. A couple cactus," Dad said. "Come on. Go to sleep. You guys are driving me crazy!"

7

BAD DREAM?

After a few minutes, Nelson fell asleep. But Winston was wide-awake. He was sure he saw something. A dark figure. Moving around by the rocks. He was scared. But he had to check it out. He climbed silently out of the truck.

Winston was shaking. But he walked

toward the rocks. Then he saw the figure of a man. No, a boy. He looked older than Winston. Around fourteen. Not very tall. With long black hair. Tanned skin. Winston stared.

The boy whistled. A beautiful black and white horse came to him. The horse had no saddle. But the boy leaped on with no problem. Was he going to ride away? No. He stopped. He saw Winston.

The boy rode toward him. Winston froze. The boy raised his hand. Was it a greeting? He said nothing. He motioned to Winston. He wanted him to climb onto the horse.

Winston had never ridden a horse before. He was scared. Horses seemed so big. So powerful. As the boy lowered his hand, Winston grabbed it. He allowed himself to be pulled up. Soon he was on the horse too. Sitting behind the boy.

Winston held on for dear life. His heart was pounding. But he was so excited. He was riding across the desert on this beautiful horse. The fear slowly melted. Excitement took over.

They rode into the dark hills. Across the sandy earth. A distant coyote howled at the full moon. There were bighorn sheep on a hillside. They did not seem bothered by the boys on the horse. A few rabbits dashed across the path.

Winston was thrilled. This was better than the best video game. What a rush!

8
RISE & SHINE

Finally, they returned to the trailhead. Winston slid off the horse. The boy handed him a small, hard object. It was wrapped in cloth. Then the boy smiled. He rode away. Winston watched him go. Then he vanished into the dark hills.

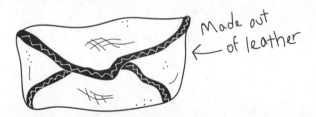

Made out of leather

Winston stuffed the cloth in his pocket. He ran back to the pickup.

Both Dad and Nelson were still sleeping.

Winston climbed into his own sleeping bag. But he couldn't sleep. He was wired. He stared at the stars. The sky turned pink with the coming dawn.

"Okay, boys," Dad said. "Time to rise and shine. Tow truck on the way. We'll be out of here soon. Maybe before sunrise." Dad pointed to the sky. "See that bright speck? Know what that is?"

"I guess an airplane. Or something," Nelson said.

Dad laughed. "That's Venus. That's another reason you guys needed this hike. You're city boys who know nothing about nature." Dad looked at Winston. "You're kinda quiet this morning."

"I'm just thinking about stuff," Winston said. He didn't know what to say. How to tell Dad and Nelson about the night. So he said nothing.

The tow truck pulled in at six. The driver fixed the truck. They were out of there before seven. They traveled the same dirt road. Bump, bump, bump. But it seemed smoother. They were going home. That made a difference.

They reached Scissors Crossing. Then headed for Julian. They stopped there for

breakfast. Pancakes. Coffee for Dad. Milk
for the boys. Everybody was hungry.

A blonde waitress said, "So, you guys
come from Ghost Mountain?"

Smells like Maple Syrup

"Sure thing," Dad said. "We had an
adventure. And then some. Didn't we, boys?"
He laughed. "We had engine trouble. Got to
spend the night in our pickup."

"It's a great place," she said. She looked
at the boys. "You have a good time hiking
with your dad?"

"I'll be glad to get home," Nelson said.

The waitress grinned. "Did you see the
ghost?" she asked.

Winston's head jerked up. "What ghost?"

"The one the mountain is named for," the waitress said. She looked at Winston. She winked. "I bet you saw him. There's a certain look you get. But only if you see him. It's in the eyes. I can tell. You got that look."

The ← Look

Winston laughed nervously. He just wasn't ready to talk about it. Maybe he never would be. He had felt so wild. So free. He had never felt that way. Until last night.

The diner wasn't too busy. The waitress had a chance to chitchat. "There's a legend. Says there's a native boy out there. Out there in the desert. A ghost boy. He rides a ghost horse. But he's only seen at night. He died a long time ago. But his spirit rides the hills. Maybe during a full moon. Maybe he visits to make sure his mountain is being taken care of. Maybe he protects it. I don't know. But that's what they say."

"I like ghost stories," Nelson said. "But to meet a real ghost? No thank you. I wouldn't want to. I'd be too scared."

9
IT WAS REAL

They finished their pancakes. Then headed out to the pickup for the ride home.

← No side of bacon, please

During the drive, Dad turned to Winston. "You been real quiet this morning. You feeling okay?"

"I'm okay," Winston said. He still wasn't ready to talk.

"Well, boys," Dad said. "We're almost home. How did you like hiking? Hanging out with your dad? What's the verdict? You have a good time?"

"My feet hurt. A lot. But it was okay," Nelson said. "I liked seeing the stars. That was cool. I guess it was fun. I mean … I'm kinda proud of myself. I did it."

Nel liked ← the stars

"Winston," Dad said. "What do you say? Did our adventure take the shine off those video games?"

"I guess so," Winston said. "Um, I was scared. Sometimes. It wasn't comfy. Not like home. But, well, the games are fun. But they're not real. This *was* real. I mean,

I feel good inside. Because we did it. And something else too, Dad. Um, that ghost? I sorta met him. Last night. When you two were asleep. It was awesome."

There, Winston thought, *I said it. I couldn't keep it a secret. Not forever. I don't care what anybody thinks. I had to say something.*

There was silence in the truck. Dead silence.

"What did you just say?" Dad asked. "I think I heard it. But I'm not sure. So tell me again. Please. And make it clear."

"Last night," Winston said slowly. "I knew I saw something. It was by the rocks." He gulped. "I was scared. But I got out of the truck. I wanted a closer look. I walked slow. And then I saw him. A kid like me. Maybe older. Fourteen? Long black hair. He looked like he belonged there. He whistled. A black and white horse came." Winston paused.

"He, uh, saw me. He seemed okay. I went closer. He got up on the horse. Didn't have a saddle. He motioned to me. Seemed like he wanted me to ride with him. He pulled me up behind him. Then we rode off."

"Wow, Winston. You had some dream. Maybe it was something you ate? Hm, maybe the pickles. That's why you had that crazy dream," Dad said.

"It wasn't a dream, Dad," Winston said. "It was real."

"It's like the waitress said. The ghost she talked about! Cool. You met him," Nelson said. "Wow! I wish it had been me."

Dad gave Nelson a playful shove. "Nah. I don't buy it. Neither should you, Nel. Don't let Winston pull our leg. It's a joke. Good one, son. Ha-ha. Wait till I tell your mom." Dad laughed.

"No joke, Dad," Winston said. "Dead serious. It was the most thrilling thing. Ever. I can't believe it. I don't know who he was. I'm not saying he was *the* ghost. Maybe he wasn't. But something happened. It happened last night. And it was real."

But Winston wasn't truly sure. Was it real? It could have been a dream. Right? The story was crazy. Wild. Impossible, really.

Soon, they were home. They pulled into the driveway. Mom came running out. It was like she was watching for them. She hugged everyone.

Mom
← waiting for
US

"Oh, you boys sure stink. I could smell you from the door. Get out of those dirty clothes. Go shower. I'll clean your stuff." Then she sighed. "It's good to have all my men home."

10
SUNSET MOUNTAIN

At dinner that night everybody talked. About the good. And the bad. About their hiking adventure. The snake. The lizard. The night sky. The stars.

Mom said the trip made dinner talk better. Before, the boys only talked about gaming. Now they talked about all sorts of things. Even their feelings.

"Oh, Winston," she said. "I almost forgot. The next level of *Doomscape*. That's your game. Right, honey? It's in the stores now. Should I buy it?"

"Uh, hold off on that, Mom," Winston said. "Let me think about it."

Dad has chicken legs

Dad slapped his knee. Then laughed. "Hey there! Color me happy," he shouted. "Didn't think I'd live to see the day."

"I'm getting older," Winston said. "Next year, I'll be in middle school. Gaming seems lame. Sometimes. I don't know. Seems like they're for little kids."

Nelson said, "Hey, Dad, where else can we hike? Do you know any other cool places? A tougher trail? Steeper? That one was sorta easy."

"Yeah," Winston said. "We need a challenge. That was too simple." Winston looked at his plate. He blushed. He felt bad because he had complained. Now he liked the idea of hiking. It was like nature was calling to him.

"Oh, Winston. I forgot to tell you." Mom started stacking plates. "Nelson, please take these to the kitchen." Then she got up. She left the dining room. Winston and his dad gave each other a look. They didn't understand women. "Hang on," she yelled from the down the hall.

When she came back, she was carrying something. "While I was sorting laundry," she said. "I found this in one of your pockets." She handed Winston a small, hard object. It was wrapped in a piece of cloth.

Winston's breath caught. His eyes got big. His hand shook. Then he took the object. How could he forget? But he had.

It was from the boy. The boy from Ghost Mountain. He opened the cloth. There was a stone with beautiful markings on it. They were just like the ones at Ghost Mountain. The markings were the same!

So it wasn't a dream. It was real. Winston couldn't explain it. But it did happen. And he would never forget it. Not for as long as he lived.

Winston looked at his father. "Dad, I'd like to go back to the Anza Borrego Desert. I want to hike again."

"You're on," Dad said. "It's a big desert. I can't wait for you kids to see Sunset Mountain."

"Hold on a sec! This time I'm coming too," Mom said. "You guys aren't keeping all the fun for yourselves. I want an adventure. Are girls allowed?"

"You bet girls are allowed," Dad said. "Especially you, Bella."

Winston and Nelson exchanged a sappy look. Their parents were weird. Nelson made loud kissing sounds. That cracked up his big brother.

Winston carried the stone to his bedroom. He put it in a special treasure box. His grandmother had given him the box. Inside were shells. From the Pacific. From the Atlantic. From the Sea of Cortez. There were also souvenirs from special places.

This stone was the most special of all.

Winston went to his window. He looked up at the sky. He had never done that before. Even in the city, he could see stars. He wanted to learn more. To know more. He grabbed a book from his desk. It has been there a long time. He started reading it.